PUFFIN BOOKS

GWENDA AND THE ANIMALS

Gwenda's first visit to the zoo with her mum, her twin brothers, her cousins and her Auntie Rosie and Uncle Mat is no fun at all. Gwenda just cannot stand the way Uncle Mat teases the animals! So at the end of the day she decides to take matters into her own hands. She won't go home – she'll stay at the zoo and see if she can help the penguins, the lions, the pandas and all the other unhappy animals. Then she discovers she has magical powers and can actually talk, and listen to her new animal friends.

How Gwenda manages to transform the zoo into a better and happier place for all the animals makes this an exciting and thought-provoking book. It will speak straight to the hearts and minds of all young animal lovers (their Uncles' too!).

Tessa Dahl was brought up in Buckinghamshire and now lives in a large household of children (three) and mongrels (two). She is a successful writer and journalist. Her articles have appeared in magazines and periodicals such as *Vogue*, *House and Garden* and *The Mail on Sunday*. Her first adult novel, *Working for Love*, and her first picture book for children, *The Same but Different*, were published within a few days of each other, and both became immediate bestsellers.

GWENDA
and the
ANIMALS

Tessa Dahl

Illustrated by Korky Paul

PUFFIN BOOKS

PUFFIN BOOKS

Published by the Penguin Group
Penguin Books Ltd, 27 Wrights Lane, London W8 5TZ, England
Penguin Books USA Inc., 375 Hudson Street, New York, New York 10014, USA
Penguin Books Australia Ltd, Ringwood, Victoria, Australia
Penguin Books Canada Ltd, 10 Alcorn Avenue, Toronto, Ontario, Canada M4V 3B2
Penguin Books (NZ) Ltd, 182–190 Wairau Road, Auckland 10, New Zealand

Penguin Books Ltd, Registered Offices: Harmondsworth, Middlesex, England

First published by Hamish Hamilton Children's Books 1989
Published in Puffin Books 1992
1 3 5 7 9 10 8 6 4 2

Filmset in Monophoto Baskerville

Printed in England by Clays Ltd, St Ives plc

CHAPTER ONE

Revolting Uncle Mat

Gwenda, her mum, her twin baby brothers Paul and Tom, her Auntie Rosie, Uncle Mat, her cousins Amy, Beth, Sarah and Ross, all went to the zoo for the day. It was wet. It was chaos. Gwenda was not happy. Her Uncle Mat was being really stupid and teasing the animals. The others thought it was funny. Gwenda did not.

At the penguin pool, Uncle Mat waddled around and the other children followed.

What twerps, thought Gwenda.

At the sea-lions, he barked and clapped his hands like flippers and the others did it too.

More like sea morons, said Gwenda to herself.

In the monkey house, Uncle Mat pretended to swing around with Ross on his back. The others scratched under their arms and screeched and squealed. The monkeys looked disgusted.

Gwenda felt disgusted. She looked at the mother monkey and whispered, 'I'm sorry, I'm so sorry.'

As she turned to leave, she heard someone say in a hushed voice, 'That's all right, we're used to it.'

I must be hearing things, she thought. The others clearly hadn't noticed anything as they lumbered about looking goofy.

In the lions' cage the lioness paced up and down. Up and down, up and down.

Uncle Mat copied her. So did Amy, Beth, Sarah and Ross. Auntie Rosie and Mum laughed. The lion yawned and watched them crossly.

'Stupid idiots,' Gwenda heard a deep voice mutter.

She looked around. There was no one else near by.

The panda bears were no better. One lay curled up on the ground and the other sat swaying to and fro.

'Hey, black eyes!' yelled Uncle Mat. 'Been in a fight? Wannanother one?'

He rolled up his sleeves and started to poke a long stick into the cage.

Gwenda could stand it no more. 'Uncle Mat, stop it. Stop teasing the animals. They're stuck in cages and you're being stupid and cruel.'

Uncle Mat swung round, furious. His face had gone purple.

'Now don't you talk to your Uncle Mat like that,' said Gwenda's mum. 'He's older and wiser than you.'

As they turned to leave Gwenda heard a little whisper.

'Older yes, wiser no, oh no.' Then a laugh.

She ran back to the cage. 'Was that you?' she asked. 'Was that really you?'

'No,' said the panda. 'Dumb animals can't talk.'

Gwenda began to tingle. Her head started to go fuzzy, as if she had hundreds of silver fish swimming inside her brain. She felt as if a dolphin was diving in her tummy. Her insides were tumbling. It was a glorious, exciting feeling, like a Roman Candle firework shooting out sparkles which zinged down her body and rolled to her toes. These were magical happenings; but best of all, she felt like she had a wonderful, beautiful bird in her chest, flapping its wings and singing.

When they arrived at the car park her mum got busy putting away the buggy and strapping the twins in their seats, while Uncle Mat loaded the other children into his car.

'Mum,' she said, 'I'm going home with the others for tea, OK?'

Gwenda's mum didn't look up. 'All right, I'll see you around six. Don't be later.'

Gwenda darted behind the parked cars. She watched Uncle Mat drive off, his car full of laughing, dirty faces, eating lollies.

Then she watched her mum go.

Well Gwenda, you've done it now, she said to herself.

· CHAPTER TWO ·

Gwenda and the Pandas

Gwenda was nimble. It was easy to duck past the ticket collector and under the turnstile.

The last of the damp visitors were milling around and she joined them, edging her way slowly back to the pandas.

When she was nearly at their cage, she took a deep breath and jumped into a rubbish bin. It was disgusting and sticky, full of the most revolting smelly things.

Dusk was setting in and she could hear the keepers shouting, 'Everyone out. Closing time.'

Her bottom was getting wet and slimy. Cripes, thought Gwenda, as she realised she was sitting on a half-eaten choc ice.

Gwenda waited. The zoo was so noisy she couldn't tell if all the people had gone. It was spooky. Birds were screaming, monkeys were screeching. The lions were roaring and something was growling.

locking up the animals stopped.

'Good-night, Bill, see you tomorrow,' she heard.

Slowly Gwenda inched her way out of the bin. She darted across the ground to the pandas' cage. They hadn't gone to bed. The panda that had been curled up was sitting chewing a piece of bamboo shoot and the panda that Gwenda had talked to was looking on.

'She's so greedy,' he said with disgust.

'What?' asked Gwenda.

'You heard me,' said the panda in a deep voice, which made Gwenda realise he was the man.

'You said she's greedy.'

'You bet she's greedy. She's a greedy pig.'

'No, I'm not, I'm a panda,' said the other panda, in a squeaky girl's voice.

'Huh, could have fooled me,' said the cross He Panda.

He moved towards Gwenda and as he did the She Panda sighed out loud, 'Sticks and stones may break my bones but words will never hurt me.'

'Talking of sticks,' grunted the He

Panda, 'your uncle was revolting today. I couldn't believe you were related to him. But I like you. Most animals – that's what we call humans – behave badly. They laugh at us or poke things through the bars. We're thoroughly disgusted by the way you animals behave.'

The She Panda was still guzzling.

'You'd better hurry up or she'll eat all your food,' warned Gwenda.

'She puts me off my food. I'll tell you

something. We pandas are from China. I lived a marvellous free life in the hills until I was captured and put in a crate, then on to a plane and brought here. In China I had my choice of wife – now

they give me her and expect us to get on. How would you like it if you were shoved in a cage and told to fall in love with some boy you'd never met before, especially if you didn't like the look of him?'

'I see your point,' said Gwenda, thinking of the most revolting boy in her class. 'But you could be nicer to her.'

'I just don't like her. We don't get on.'

'Have you tried?' asked Gwenda.

'No, he has not,' chipped in the She Panda. 'He's been horrid to me. I'm homesick and lonely and . . .'

'Are you? You didn't tell me that.' The He Panda sounded surprised.

'Well, you never asked. In fact in six months you've hardly spoken to me.'

'Is that true?' said Gwenda.

The He Panda looked a bit guilty and didn't answer.

'I said is that true?' asked Gwenda in her strictest voice.

'Well, all she does is eat,' he grumbled.

'I only eat because I'm bored.'

'Look,' said Gwenda, 'I think you two have a lot of talking to do. No one just gets on. Often you have to work at it. Even people who have been married for years have to try.'

'Have a bamboo shoot.' The She Panda held out her paws to the grumpy He Panda.

'Well, I might just do that.' He moved a bit closer to her. 'I never noticed before, but you've got lovely eyes,' he said.

Gwenda smiled. 'Good-night,' she whispered.

'Good-night, Gwenda,' they answered.

She started to walk away. As she turned the corner she looked back and smiled. The pandas didn't notice; they were busy.

CHAPTER THREE

The Penguins Protest

Gwenda was very happy about the pandas. So she did a little dance. She wasn't worried about her mum or how cross she would be. She wasn't frightened of the dark or the noises. I have magic, she said to herself. Something extraordinary, something peculiar is happening to me. I can help these animals. They are my friends.

She walked past the monkey house. All was quiet. Gwenda knew they had been locked up for the night.

'Sleep well, marvellous monkeys,' she called, and blew them a kiss.

The penguins were nestling down, getting ready to sleep.

'Hello, chaps,' said Gwenda.

'Oy, oy, oy. Who have we here?' asked a big penguin. Gwenda realised he was the chief.

'Yes, yes, yes. Who have we here?' echoed the others.

'I'm Gwenda.'

'Shouldn't you be at home with your animal relations?' asked the chief.

'I'd rather be here,' said Gwenda.

'We wouldn't,' said the chief.

'Oh no, no, no we wouldn't,' said the others. 'We come from the beautiful South Pole where we have thousands of miles of icy land to live on. Sharp blue sea to swim in, ice hills to slide down and fresh fish to dive for.'

'Fish, fish, fresh fish to dive for,' sang the others longingly.

'But we're here and we don't complain. We have no choice.'

'No choice, no choice, we have no choice . . .'

Gwenda noticed how sadly they whispered this.

'But there is one thing that bothers us. It makes us miserable. It fills us with fear and rattles our bones.'

'What's that?' Gwenda was aching to know.

'Every day at tea-time we have to do the Penguin Parade. It's stupid, we feel stupid.'

'Stupid, stupid, we feel stupid,' muttered the others.

'We are marched through the zoo to the pool where we are fed. Everyone laughs at us. People even film us with cameras. No one laughed at us walking in the South Pole. What right have they to laugh, those ugly human animals who are fat or skinny, who have odd shapes and come in different colours? At least we all look the same.'

'I agree, it's shocking,' said Gwenda.

'But that's not it, it's far worse,' said the chief.

'Far worse, far worse,' nodded the other penguins.

'When we reach the elephants they

make us turn right. We hate it. We try and turn left, but they make us turn right. It rattles our bones.'

'Rattles our bones, rattles our bones,' the penguins said with a judder.

'But what, what is it, what terrible thing happens if you turn right?'

'Right is wrong,' said the chief. 'Because down that path are the wolves.'

'Aren't they in cages?' asked Gwenda.

'It's not enough.'

'Not enough, not enough,' the penguins added, shaking their heads.

'Those wolves are evil, bad wolves.

They say terrible things to us.'

'Like what?' gasped Gwenda.

'Well, as we get closer they start to shout, "Here comes lunch, penguin burgers, get

out the nosebag!" Then they move to the front of their cages and by the time we get near they are whispering, their horrible sharp teeth shining while they slobber, "We're going to get you. We're going to creep out tonight and munch you up." And as their voices get louder they taunt, "We'll sneak out of our cages, we know where you are, and you won't hear us *until it's too late*." They always make us jump when they shout that bit at the end. And then they laugh. Oh it's horrible, they upset us so much. Can you help us, Gwenda?'

Gwenda thought for a moment. Then her back started to tingle as if a tiny koala bear was crawling up her spine. Suddenly she felt the wonderful, beautiful bird in her chest flapping its wings again.

'Yes, oh yes,' she said. 'Of course I can. Good-night, penguins, you can sleep well tonight. I'll protect you from the wolves.'

CHAPTER FOUR

Missing Cubs

The light was disappearing. Gwenda knew she did not have much time. Once it was dark the animals would be going to sleep.

Gwenda also knew that her mum would soon be wondering where she was. Then there'd be trouble.

For a moment she felt frightened. Should she stop now and see if she could find a way home? Perhaps she should find a keeper and pretend she'd been left behind.

But then she remembered the animals, her animals, and knew she had to keep going.

Suddenly as if from nowhere the bats started to swoop around. She watched them shoot through the sky and drop down into the penguin pool, like swallows.

Then they would soar up again towards the stars. As she stood trying to make up her mind a bat skimmed past her head.

'Don't give up, Gwenda,' it whispered, and off it sped.

Again, as if a dart had whizzed past her ear, another bat came, getting so close it made her hair rustle.

'Go to the lions, they need you,' it squeaked.

'Hang on,' gasped Gwenda, but the bat had shot into the sky.

THESE ANIMALS
ARE HIGHLY
DANGEROUS

THE MALE LION IS NAMED
·ZIMBA·
THE FEMALE IS NAMED
·ZELDA·

CUBS CAN BE SEEN AT
THE CHILDREN'S ZOO
THESE LIONS ARE FROM
·AFRICA·

Gwenda did not stop to think. She ran. She ran past the sea-lions, and as she sped she heard them clapping their flippers and barking, 'Go on Gwenda, go on.'

She did not stop. Her feet felt as if they had become the hooves of a little gazelle, light and delicate. Her legs seemed to glide. And there it was, right in front of her: the lions' cage.

'About time too,' said the lion.

Gwenda read the sign on the bars:

'What does it say, Gwenda, what does the sign say?' asked Zimba.

'It says your cubs can be seen in the children's zoo.'

Zelda started to cry. She roared and shook and sobbed. 'They're alive, Zimba. Oh my darling, they are alive, I knew they were.'

Zimba started to lick Zelda's face lovingly.

'My darling, my dearest, it's all right. It will be all right. Believe me, we'll get them back, Gwenda will help us.

'Oh, Gwenda, we have had such troubled times. My poor Zelda gave birth to twin cubs a few days ago. We were so happy. We had longed for them. For a day she mothered them, loved them and fed them. We named them Harry and Mary and we were proud. Oh, so proud.'

With this Zelda roared again. Such a sad, empty noise.

Zimba went on: 'But the keeper came, he gave us each an injection and we went all woozy. When we woke up Harry and Mary were gone. Since then our lives have been misery. My little love Zelda has paced up and down, up and down. She will not eat, she will not sleep. She cries for her babies.'

'This is terrible,' said Gwenda feeling the tears falling down her cheeks. 'Oh, Zimba, I must help you.'

'Not only am I worried about our twins, but I am fearful for Zelda. We come from Kenya, in Africa. We had hundreds of miles of golden land to live in. We were so happy. Zelda and I were free. It was hot and beautiful. It was our kingdom. In Africa Zelda had many cubs and she was a good mother. But we were captured and put in cages and brought here. We have done our best. We have no choice. We had each other and our love. We have managed behind bars, in the cold. We have never complained. But now we have been cheated.'

Gwenda shuddered. She tried to imagine how she would feel if someone took her away from her cosy little home and her friends and flew her to a strange country; if she were put into a cage. Even worse, she tried to imagine a person giving her mum an injection and taking away the twins. Gwenda started to get angry. She heard hundreds of bees buzzing in her head. Her fingers started to wriggle like little worms. She felt as if she had a shark in her tummy. Her insides were tumbling with fury, rockets were shooting around her heart.

Gwenda knew she had to help. She realised her magic had been given to her for a reason. It was not for fun. To have this amazing wonderful power was a gift and now she had to use it. This was serious.

Zimba looked at her. There were tears in his eyes, too.

'Gwenda, oh Gwenda, please help us!'

'I will, oh yes I will,' she answered.

CHAPTER FIVE

Gwenda to the Rescue

Bill was not happy. He loved his animals and he was worried. Bill had been head keeper at the zoo for a long time. Things had changed. People seemed to want to be amused by the animals. Bill did not like that. He could remember the days when everyone

seemed happy to admire them. But now that was not enough. Bill knew the animals should not be used to entertain people, but he also knew he had a job to do. He had to keep the crowds coming, but Bill did not want to hurt the animals.

As he made his tea that night, in his little cottage by the zoo gates, he felt sad. Why don't people love the animals?

he thought. How can I keep doing this job when I have to keep finding ways to entertain the humans? As he poured himself a mug of tea he thought he saw a little girl walk past his window. Come on Bill, he said to himself, you're tired, perhaps it's all getting too much and I should give up and go and live by the seaside. But then what would happen to my animals? He shuddered. He rubbed his eyes and looked again. No, he wasn't seeing things. Coming up his path there was a little girl.

He heard a knock on the door. Whatever next, thought Bill as he turned the key, opened the door; and there stood Gwenda. Bill felt peculiar. He looked at Gwenda. All around her she had a huge circle of tiny flames, as if there were hundreds of matches glowing behind her little body. She seemed to be one enormous firework, with beautiful sparks and coloured waterfalls shooting out around her. Straight away Bill knew this tiny person, this small child, was very important. He couldn't work out why or how but all of a sudden in one enormous rush the tiredness and sadness left him and he started to smile. Then he giggled and the

giggling turned to laughter. He roared with laughter and Gwenda started laughing, too. Then Bill put his hand out and took Gwenda's; and as he touched her he felt a glow, and a shot of electricity went through him like a bolt of lightning.

Laughing, they went into his little sitting-room. Then Gwenda stopped laughing.

'Your lions are miserable,' she said.

'I know,' sighed Bill.

'Your penguins are terrified.'

'I know,' said Bill. 'They are losing their feathers and I don't know what to do about it.'

'I do,' said Gwenda. 'What's more, I know your lady panda is eating too much and your male not enough.'

'You're right,' said Bill. 'There is such sadness in my zoo.'

'You're not helping it,' said Gwenda.

Bill looked down at this little squirt of a girl. How does she know these things, he thought. But he also had a feeling that he should not ask or argue.

'Gwenda, I have problems. I have a man who owns the zoo, who wants to make more money.'

'He won't make more money if his animals are unhappy,' replied Gwenda. 'His animals will not have babies, they'll lose their feathers, they'll starve to death. Then he won't make money.'

'I know you're right,' said Bill quietly.

'How would you like to be them? Put yourself in their cages for a few days. You'd soon see, and Bill, it's up to you, no one else can or will help. I'm sure we can come up with nicer tricks to make money for your zoo, but first you must promise you will always keep me and my words a secret.'

'I promise,' said Bill.

'And also you must help me out of a spot of bother with my mum. Will you call her up and say you found me crying in the car park because the others had driven off without me?'

Gwenda told Bill her telephone number. He dialled it and spoke to her mum.

'I'm glad I called, as she was beginning to get worried.

She's on her way and she's very relieved,' said Bill.

'Now please let me talk, and you listen, Bill,' said Gwenda.

'Did you take away Zelda's cubs?'

'Yes,' said Bill, looking guilty.

'Do you make your penguins go and parade for their supper?'

'Yes, I'm afraid I do.'

'Do you make them turn right by the wolves and do they always try to turn left?'

'Yes,' gasped Bill, amazed.

'Well, you should have thought about it more,' said Gwenda. 'It's your job to think for the animals. Did you put the lady panda straight into the panda cage without giving them time to get to know each other slowly?'

'But it's money, Gwenda. It's money and time. Mr Mollyskin, the man who owns the zoo, wanted the pandas to hurry and have babies to draw the crowds. He wanted to make the penguins parade to make people laugh. He made me take Zelda's cubs to the children's zoo, so we could get more people in to watch them being bottle fed.'

'OK, Bill, but we can make it change. I know we can. The animals love you – you are the only person they have to protect them, so they need you more than Mr Mollyskin does. We'll keep Mr Mollyskin happy, but your job is to protect

your animals. Like mums and dads with their children.'

While Bill made Gwenda a mug of cocoa and a huge cheese sandwich, Gwenda told Bill why his pandas were not having babies. She told him that the penguins were in fear of their lives and how to change it. She warned him of Zelda's deep unhappiness and how he must give the lion cubs back to Zimba and Zelda.

Bill never asked Gwenda how she knew these things. He knew better.

'I promise you, Gwenda, from tomorrow I'll change it, I'll change it all.'

'Now, Mr Mollyskin will like this idea,' said Gwenda. 'It's a corker.'

As Gwenda munched away at her enormous sandwich she told Bill of a way the zoo could make lots of money.

'You build a cage, an empty cage. Then you put up a sign in front of the zoo saying that the zoo expects people to treat the animals kindly and respect their happiness. Anyone found being cruel or making fun of the animals will have the same thing done to them. Then you make sure that the keepers guard the animals, and the minute you catch an idiot being nasty you bang them straight in the special cage. It will work wonderfully. Gosh, on Sundays and holidays the

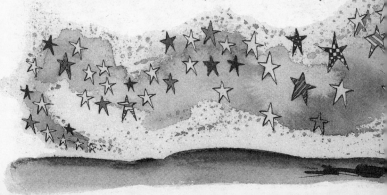

cages will be packed. Then other people will come to see and make fun of the bullies.

'The zoo will be crammed with happy animals and with any luck it will end up with people making fun of people.'

'Mr Mollyskin will love the idea,' shouted Bill. 'Hurrah, you're a magician.'

Gwenda smiled, and as she did Bill could swear he could hear the magical sound of a huge bird flapping its wings, and he saw flashes of light like sparklers come from Gwenda's eyes.

Nowadays, Uncle Mat does not go to the zoo. He did not enjoy his last visit, when

he found himself in a cage with a crowd of people laughing at him and the monkeys in the cage opposite copying his every move.

But Gwenda goes to the zoo a lot. She often gets a telephone call from Bill, asking her to visit and sort out a problem.

'Gwenda,' he says, 'I think we need a bit of advice.'

And Gwenda always goes in when the

crowds have gone home. She chats to Zelda and Zimba and their family, gossips with the penguins, admires the pandas' baby; and all her animal friends share their worries with her. Even the wolves have stopped calling her 'Little Red Riding Hood', and try to be polite when she passes.

If there's a problem that Bill has missed, the bats always lead her to it.

When she's finished her business, Gwenda knocks on Bill's door. Together they sit while Gwenda eats a huge cheese sandwich with a mug of cocoa, and they talk about the animals.

Some other Young Puffin Read Alones

PINK SOCKS and GREEN GLOVES
Angela Bull

With one week to go, Robin is worried that he will never find a suitable present for his sister Lucy's birthday, but then he stumbles upon the perfect pink present and he is determined to buy it. In the second story, Lucy finds some hilarious uses for an unwanted present – a pair of very bright green felt gloves!

A GINGER CAT AND A SHAGGY DOG
Pamela Oldfield

As a kitten, Ginger is always getting into trouble: nearly drowned in the fishpond; almost run over by a bicycle; even lost for four days. Somehow he survives, but what will happen when he's used up all nine of his lives?

In the second story, poor Ginger has a dog to contend with. When Shaggy arrives at the front gate, Timmy thinks he is the answer to all his dreams. But then his new neighbour, Sarah, comes looking for a dog *she* calls Bruno. Will Timmy have to give up Shaggy after all?

BLESSU and DUMPLING
Dick King-Smith

Poor Dumpling. All she wants is to be as sleek and long as her brothers, to look as a dachshund should look. Then she meets a witch's cat who grants her wish – and Dumpling discovers that length isn't everything!

Blessu the baby elephant doesn't need a magic spell to make his trunk grow longer – it happens when he sneezes. And for an elephant with hayfever, that makes life very uncomfortable indeed . . .

Dick King-Smith has created two more adorable animal characters in these very funny stories for young children.

GERTIE'S GANG

Margaret Joy

In the playground or the classroom, life for Gertie's Gang is always full of fun. There are games to play, errands to run, a rabbit to find, and even a wolf to hunt in these six lively stories.

ERIC'S ELEPHANT AND OTHER STORIES

John Gatehouse et al

Eric had always wanted a pet of his own, but not an elephant! And Eric knows it will be difficult to convince his mother that an elephant is the best pet in the world.

Eric's Elephant is just one of the four hilarious animal stories from four top story-tellers, here for the first time in one volume. In the other three stories you can meet Mouse Mad Madeline, an unpredictable dog called Benbow and a family who have every kind of pet – except the one they really want.

JIM HEDGEHOG AND
THE SUPERNATURAL CHRISTMAS

Russell Hoban

Lots of people like a little snack while watching the telly. Just be sure you stay on the right side of the screen. Readers and TV addicts of all ages will enjoy this tasty thriller starring Jim Hedgehog and the Revolting Blob.

DODIE

Finola Akister

Dodie the dachshund lives with Miss Smith and Tigercat in a country cottage. He has all sorts of adventures, because he's a very special dog. He is very good at finding things. He finds Miss Smith's key when she gets locked out, he finds Tigercat's new kitten, and he even finds a prickly hedgehog! Life is never dull for Dodie.

HERE COME THE TWINS

Beverly Cleary

Twins are full of surprises: just ask Mr Lemon, the postman. Janet and Jimmy can turn anything into a game, whether it's getting their first grown-up beds, or going to buy new shoes. But what will they do when their next-door neighbour gives them each a dog biscuit? Give them to a dog? No, that would be too easy!

THE FRIDAY PARCEL

Ann Pilling

Two highly enjoyable stories in which Matt goes to stay on his own with Gran-in-the-country, and sets his heart on buying a lion at the jungle sale.

STICK TO IT, CHARLIE

Joy Allen

In these two 'Charlie' adventures, Charlie meets a new friend and finds a new interest – playing the piano. The new friend proves his worth when Charlie and the gang find themselves in a tight spot. As for the piano, well, even football comes second place!

THE LITTLE EXPLORER

Margaret Joy

The little explorer is setting out on a long voyage. He is going in search of the pinkafrillia, the rarest flower in the world. Together with Knots, the sailor, and Peckish, the parrot, Stanley journeys through the jungle of Allegria – and what adventures they have!

THE SCHOOL POOL GANG

Geraldine Kaye

Billy is the head of the Back Lane Gang and he's always coming up with good ideas. So when money is needed for a new school pool, his first idea is to change the gang's name. His next idea – to raise money by giving donkey rides – leads to all sorts of unexpected and exciting happenings!

DUSTBIN CHARLIE

Ann Pilling

Charlie has always liked seeing what people threw out in their dustbins. So he's thrilled to find the toy of his dreams among the rubbish in the skip. But during the night, someone else takes it. The culprit in this highly enjoyable story turns out to be the most surprising person.

CLASS THREE AND THE BEANSTALK

Martin Waddell

Two unusual stories which will amaze you. Class Three's project of growing things gets out of hand after they plant a packet of Jackson's Giant Bean seeds. And when Wilbur Small is coming home, the whole street is buzzing – except for Tom Grice and his family, who are new in the street so don't know what the fuss is about, or why people are so nervous!

THE TWIG THING

Jan Mark

As soon as Rosie and Ella saw the house they knew that something was missing. It had lots of windows and stairs, but where was the garden? When they move in, they find a twig thing which they put in water on the window-sill, and gradually things begin to change.